Hillel Takes a Bath

By **Vicki L. Weber**

Illustrated by **John Joven**

This **PJ BOOK** belongs to

_____

_____

PJ *Library*®

JEWISH BEDTIME STORIES and SONGS

APPLES & HONEY PRESS

For Rebecca, Joel, and Ben, in memory of both happy bath times
and happy story times. —VLW

To God; my Mom and Dad; my beloved teachers along my life. —JJ

Apples & Honey Press

An imprint of Behrman House
Behrman House, Millburn, NJ 07041

www.applesandhoneypress.com

ISBN 978-1-68115-546-3

LIBRARY OF CONGRESS CATALOGING-IN-PUBLICATION DATA
Names: Weber, Vicki L., 1956- author. | Joven, John, illustrator.
Title: Hillel takes a bath / by Vicki L. Weber ; illustrated by John Joven.
Description: [Millburn, NJ] : Apples & Honey Press, an imprint of Behrman
   House, [2019] | "Hillel, the Talmudic sage, has some wise advice for his
   students"--Provided by publisher. | Includes bibliographical references
   and index.
Identifiers: LCCN 2018015157 | ISBN 9781681155463 (alk. paper)
Subjects: LCSH: Hillel, active 1st century B.C.--1st century A.D.--Juvenile
   literature. | Commandments (Judaism)--Juvenile literature.
Classification: LCC BM755.H45 W43 2019 | DDC 296.1/20092--dc23 LC record available at https://lccn.loc.gov/2018015157

The illustrations were created using digital tools.

Design by Zahava Bogner

Edited by Ann D. Koffsky

Printed in China

9 8 7 6 5 4 3 2 1

101927.7K1/B1454/A5

Rabbi Hillel came to school one day with a large linen cloth on his shoulder and a twinkle in his eye.

"Today I will use this cloth to do a mitzvah," he said to his class.

He whisked the cloth off his shoulder and snapped it in the air.

"What do you think I will do?"

The rabbi's students were puzzled and delighted.

They never knew from one day to the next what their teacher would do in order to help them learn to follow God's ways.

Why, one time a man challenged Rabbi Hillel to teach the whole Torah to him while he balanced on one foot—and their wise and mischievous teacher had accepted the challenge!

"Do unto others as you would have others do unto you," Rabbi Hillel had told the man.

"That is the whole Torah. Now, go and study."

The man had sheepishly put his foot back down and signed up for some classes!

The students whispered together to find an answer.

"Will you give it to a poor man to use as a blanket?" asked one.

"Giving tzedakah is an important mitzvah," said Rabbi Hillel.

"It reminds us that everyone deserves justice and mercy in God's world. But that is not what I will do with this cloth today."

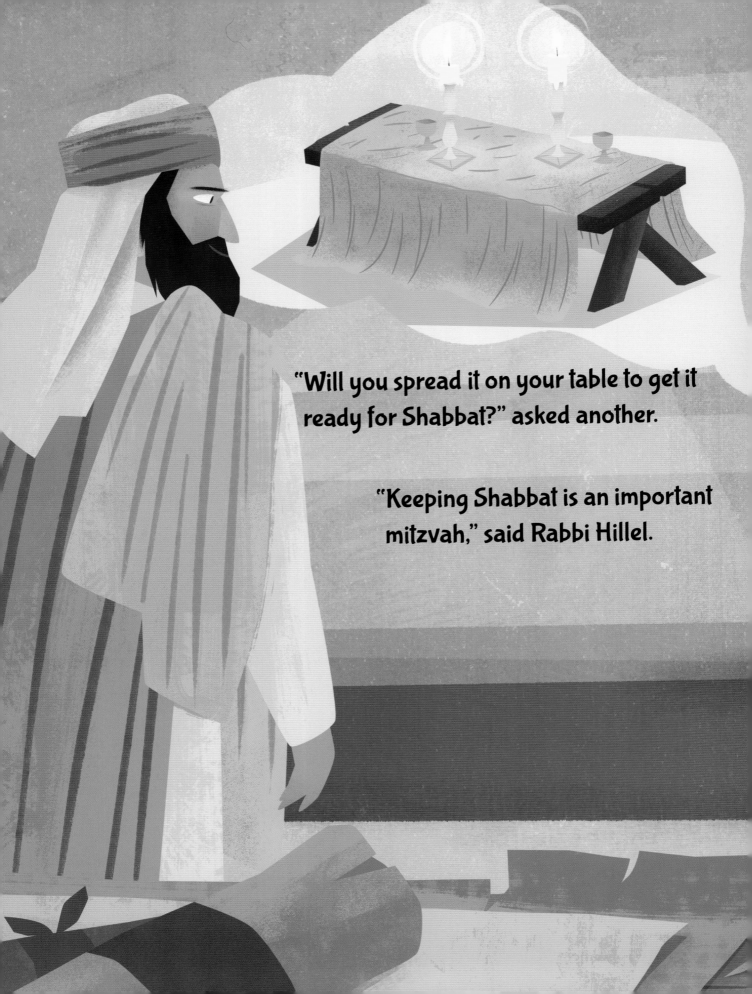

"Will you spread it on your table to get it ready for Shabbat?" asked another.

"Keeping Shabbat is an important mitzvah," said Rabbi Hillel.

"It reminds us that we must keep our holy day special to honor God. But that is not what I will do with this cloth today."

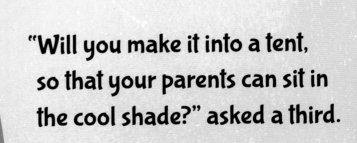

"Will you make it into a tent, so that your parents can sit in the cool shade?" asked a third.

"Honoring one's parents is an important mitzvah," said Rabbi Hillel.

"It reminds us of everything that God commanded at Mount Sinai. But that is not what I will do with this cloth today."

The students thought and talked. They talked and thought.

For each new answer,
Rabbi Hillel praised them
for thinking of an important
mitzvah.

But each time, Hillel would
tell them, "But that is not what
I will do with this cloth today."

At last, the students could think of nothing more.

"Tell us, Rabbi," they pleaded.
"What other mitzvah can you
possibly do with your cloth?"

"Ahh," said Rabbi Hillel.

"Today I will use
this cloth to dry myself
after I take a bath."

"Take a bath!" exclaimed
the surprised students.

"How can taking a
bath be a mitzvah?"

"Ahh," said Rabbi Hillel.

"Let's think about that while we take a walk."

Rabbi Hillel picked up his cloth and led his students out of the classroom.

They walked through the city until they came to the marketplace.

It was an open, busy plaza where people of the city came every day to buy and sell and conduct their business.

"Look," Rabbi Hillel said to his students.

"Tell me what you see at the end of the plaza."

"It is a statue of the king," said one of the students.

"And what are the workers doing?" asked Rabbi Hillel.

"They are cleaning the statue," said another student.

"And why do you think the workers are cleaning the statue of the king?" Rabbi Hillel asked.

"Well," said one student, "the statue is made in the image of the king. If the people allowed it to become dirty, it would show lack of respect for the king."

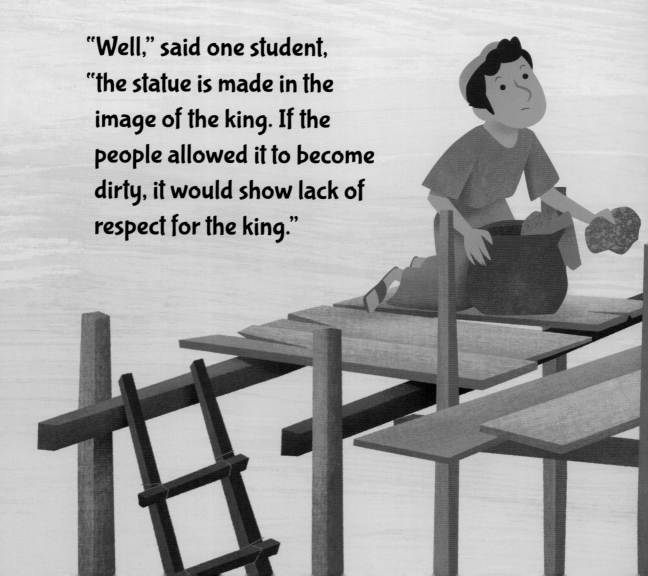

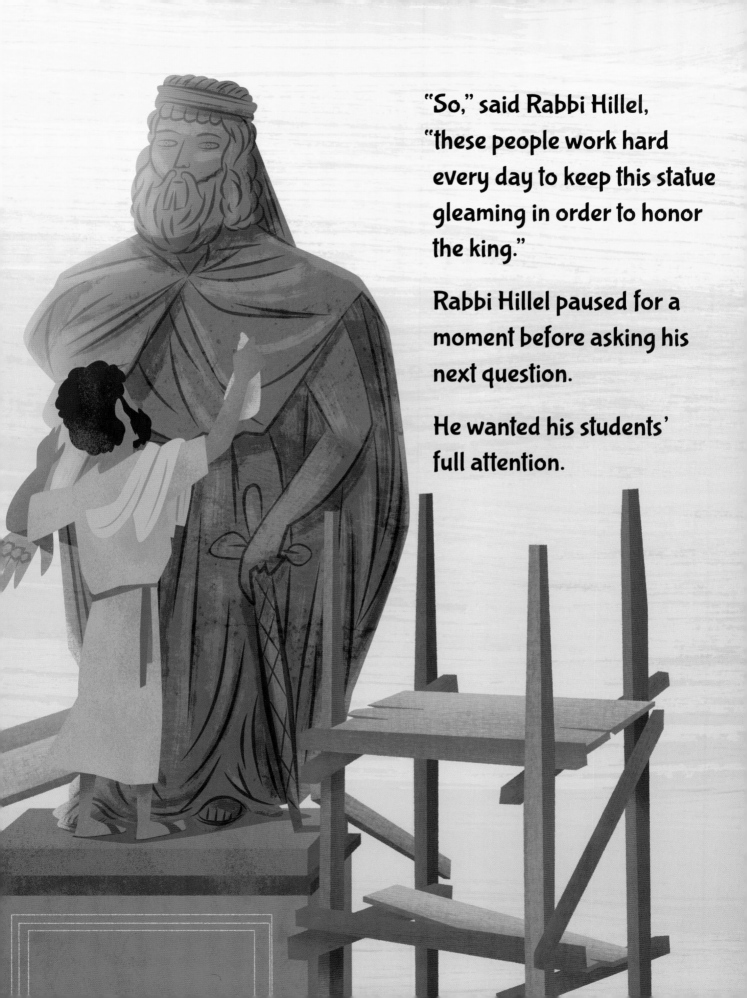

"So," said Rabbi Hillel, "these people work hard every day to keep this statue gleaming in order to honor the king."

Rabbi Hillel paused for a moment before asking his next question.

He wanted his students' full attention.

"And in whose image are we made, you and I?" he asked.

All the students answered together, for they had learned this lesson well. "We are made in God's image."

"Yes!" said Rabbi Hillel.

"So how can I use this cloth to honor God?"

"You can take a bath!" the students laughed.

"Right!" said Rabbi Hillel.

"When we keep ourselves clean, we honor God. And that is why taking a bath is an important mitzvah."

Rabbi Hillel smiled at his students
and sent them home.

And then he went
to take his bath.

Note for Families

Did you know that Hillel was a real person? He was a kind and gentle teacher, and Jewish tradition tells many stories about him. Some of the stories explain how much he loved Torah; others describe how thoughtful he would be when teaching others about a mitzvah.

A mitzvah is a commandment, one of 613 specific acts described in the Torah. Today, the word mitzvah has come to also mean an act of human kindness.

There are several *mitzvot* mentioned in this story, including giving to the poor, keeping Shabbat . . . and taking a bath! Taking a bath is a mitzvah because it is a Jewish value to be kind to ourselves, too.

- How do you take care of yourself?
- What act of kindness has someone done for you?
- What act of kindness have you done for someone else?

With kindness,